She.
And I

Angela
Beastall

About the author

A postie firmly in the middle of a mid-life crisis, that's how Angela's husband puts it anyway.

Angela Beastall is a fifty-two-year-old postwoman. She started her working life in the factories of the early 90s when the job market was just starting to stagnate. Redundancy led her towards a different career choice and so she spent twenty plus years in procurement and stock control, before completely changing her career and becoming a postwoman. She lives in Derbyshire with her husband to whom she has been married to for twenty-seven years. Writing a book has always been on her bucket list, and here it is. Me, She and I is her debut novella.

First Edition 2022

Copyright ©Angela Beastall

Her life was a little crowded...

The Husband

The Lover

The Third Man

All mixing with the ghosts of her past.

It was a journey she was compelled to take, the desire building within too strong to keep her on a safe path.

Her life was already littered with broken pieces, mostly hers, but this time she wanted more, didn't she?

A question posed?

Would she find an answer on her journey of self-discovery towards the dark desires rising within?

Eventually the shadows catch up with us all.

Contents Page

Book One

ME

What's in

What's in a tear as it forms
All your hopes
All your dreams
Gone in the blink of an eye

What's in your mind as you wake from your sleep
All your worry
All your fear
Brighter in the light of day

What's in your heart as you breathe
All your love
All your faith
Growing stronger with every breath

What's in a life and what is it for
To Live
To Love
To be

©Angie Beastall

A question posed

"So," her lover's voice broke through her silent contemplation, "why do you need someone else when you have me and your husband?"

It was a question that she had asked herself countless times, up to yet she was unable to find an answer, well, not an answer she could share with her lover if she was being entirely honest with herself. Watching him place the tray down on the table in front of her, she leant across and removed her glass of soya iced latte along with his tall mug of tea placing them both on the table. Once empty he put the tray on the half wall at the side of where they liked to sit. Her eyes stayed on him as he sat in the tub chair opposite hers. Picking up her drink she leant back into comfort of the high-backed green winged chair that was her favourite, raising the latte with her left hand she took the straw in her right, putting it between her lips she tasted the coolness of her favourite coffee shop tipple that was the epitome of a summer's day. Turning her head to look out of the large bay window of the coffee shop, she silently watched the world go by, her mind switched on as to how to answer the question posed. The world outside was going about its business, oblivious to the turmoil that was invading her head. It was her favourite spot, truthfully, they both loved the spot, it was good for people watching, well that and it wasn't conspicuous if any of their work colleagues walked by.

Turning to once more look at the man sat opposite her, she peered over the top of the glass as she slowly drank the liquid, her eyes meeting those of her lover.

"Are you going to answer me?" he questioned his gaze holding hers.

Taking another long leisurely drink before breaking eye contact as she slowly placed her glass once more on the table, crossing her left leg over her right, she crossed her forearms over the top of her now crossed legs resting them on her raised knee. Leaning forward, "Does it matter?" she questioned him her voice low. She smiled across at him hoping he would let the matter drop, knowing that he wouldn't until he was satisfied in his own mind.

"Not really," came the reply, "but if it doesn't matter why are you hesitant to answer?"

Fuck she thought, he got me there. Outwardly she laughed, "true," she replied, the laughter clear in her voice. Moving her hand across the space between them he reached out towards her outstretched hand, their fingers touched, it was the briefest of touches, but it meant everything to them both. They were friends, best friends, they had no trouble showing their affection for each other in public. The coffee shop and its sights and sounds faded into oblivion; it became just the two of them once more. The first two or the last two on earth, they knew not nor cared.

Just us

Take your hand and place it over my eyes
Ask the question
What do you see?
I see nothing, but dream of everything

Take your hand and place it on my neck
What do you feel?
I feel you, I feel me, I feel us

Take your hand and place it on my heart
Ask the question
Who does it beat for?
It beats to live, to love, to be

©Angie Beastall

A noisy group entered the coffee shop knocking into their table breaking the silent understanding that passed between them. Uncrossing her legs, she once more leant back into the comfort of the high-back chair, closing her eyes, she took a deep breath before once more opening her eyes to look directly into her lovers' questioning ones.

"OK," she sighed, "I will try to answer your question," wiggling a little in the chair to find the perfect spot as she spoke. Once the spot was found she reached across to retrieve her drink once more, mainly to use as a comfort blanket, and even as a barrier between them. Staring down into the contents of the tall glass she mindlessly stirred her latte with the straw, trying to gather her thoughts as she watched the ice swirling around chinking on the sides of the glass, staring at it for a moment longer before lifting her eyes to meet his once more.

"I know why," her voice filled with the sorrow that was rising within, "but it's hard trying to put it into words." Closing her eyes to stop the tears that she could feel brewing, she didn't want to disappoint the man sat in front of her by revealing what was occurring between her and the third man. She hadn't gone out looking for someone else, it was never meant to happen, it just had. She opened her eyes to see the concern in the eyes of her lover as the threatened tears turned her blue eyes shiny.

"Stop," his concern growing, "if it upsets you, stop!"

"These tears aren't just for me, they are for both of us, for the hurt I have caused and for the hurt I know I have yet to cause." She knew there was a journey ahead, a dark journey to reach a destination as yet unknown, even to her, a journey she must take to its conclusion.

"Then don't tell me," concern growing in his voice as he reached across to take her hand in his, "just as you don't want to hurt me, I don't want to cause you pain." Lifting her hand to his lips he gently turned her hand over and kissed her palm before placing it over his heart, "Who does it beat for," he whispered?

She was on the verge of losing control at the gentle gesture from her forgiving lover. "But" a thought rose within her mind, "just how much and what would he forgive her for?"

It was a question that she didn't want to find out. Just as she didn't want her husband finding out about her. Not just about the current life she was living, but also about the abuse she had suffered throughout her childhood, or the countless lovers she had taken before she had met and married him.

Her young single lifestyle had inevitably led to a pregnancy. She was nineteen when she had been caught out, turning her world upside down, leaving her devastated. Intuitively knowing that she did not want to bring a child into this world, into her world. The foetus' father was sixteen years older than her and a divorcee with two children. She knew how much he loved and missed his children; he had been pleased that she was carrying his unborn child. But he was a drunk who spent most of his waking hours in the local pub. They didn't see each other in the week as she worked in the day and spent most weeknights catching up with friends, going to the local cinema or seeing family. They were a weekend couple only and that suited them both, she had never asked nor wanted anything more from him. When he turned up the following weekend with a younger model in tow, it had upset and angered her. She had once more been on the brunt end of hurt and humiliation, and she was tired of being on the receiving end. The revenge she had enacted on him had been cruel and calculating. Not only had she destroyed him by telling him she had aborted his child, but she had also laughed in his face as she turned and walked out of his life. It was strange, she hadn't thought about that point in her life for many years, she wasn't proud of how cruel she had been, but she had no regrets. It made her wonder why this memory featured strongly in her mind when she thought about the third man that had recently entered her life.

"I need to tell you," She whispered, "because hopefully it will help me to further understand me," hesitating a little before she continued, "There is nothing I won't tell you if you ask the right question, and if there's a truthful answer within me that wouldn't cause you to suffer." Moving forward in her chair to get closer to him, she reached across and ran her fingers through his short strawberry blond hair, stopping at the base of his neck, she pulled him closer "I love you; you know that don't you?" she questioned looking directly into his brown eyes.

"Yes," his strained voice replied

"Do you remember that day in the office when I first told you that I loved you?" she continued, the memory and the pain from that day still raw within her.

"Yes," he lowered his head remembering the shock that she must have seen etched across his features.

She had borne her soul that day by telling him how she felt, which didn't happen very often. She had reached out to him, and he had crushed her. "I won't tell you again," she had told him as she lowered her arm and walked back behind the desk, putting a barrier between them once more. His cold reply of "Good" had cemented within her that she felt more for him than he did her. "Well, your face that day said it all, that was when it all changed for me," she lowered her head to hide a new onslaught of tears that threatened. To her tears were a sign of weakness, she hated to fucking cry, but she really hated to cry in front of anyone, it made her vulnerable, she thought herself stronger than that. "I loved you too much," lowering her head a little, trying to compose her thoughts before she continued, "I never had any intention of telling you just how much you hurt me that day, but in order for me to try to explain the reasoning behind my actions, I needed to tell you. Because of the hurt a part of me closed off from you that day, to avoid more pain, and in doing so it caused a void." She looked at him the shock clear to see on her lovers' face.

"Don't," he whispered.

"I have to," she responded, "That is where it started." Reaching across she took his hand. "That was then, this is now, always remember that" her voice filled with the pain that she had felt that day. "We are all fragile in our own way, it doesn't matter how strong we say we are or appear to be, but the void your rejection left needed to be filled."

Pulling away from her the shock and anger clear not only on his face, but in his voice, "So you're saying this is my fault?"

"Not at all," she looked down at the floor, at her shoes, looking anywhere but at her lover. She didn't want to see the disappointment; the anger and shock were enough. "But" her voice imploring him, "you have to understand me to understand this, and to understand this you need to know everything, the only thing is," she paused before continuing, "I'm not sure that I am capable of telling you everything."

"Why not?" he questioned, "I'm confused, you tell me you need to tell me everything, then tell me you can't in the same breath!"

"I know," bowing her head once more, "I can't tell you, because I haven't even worked me out yet," she raised her hands and shrugged. "Shall I continue?"

Give and take

A new chapter to write
But where to begin!
Start with a statement
End with a kiss
The middle is where it is
Actions, hurts and desires fulfilled
Take what you want
Give what you must
Locked together in bondage
Surfeit, fruition, sated

©Angie Beastall

She remembered back to the first day she had started her new job, the excitement at beginning a new chapter in her life. It was a job she had always wanted to do; she classed it as her road to retirement. The third man had been in her eyeline from the very start, but she hadn't changed her lifestyle to find distractions or turmoil. She had wanted a change of pace, a gentler pace. She needed to create an empty space for her mind to rebuild itself. She knew the work would be manual, hard work had never scared her, after all, she had started her work life in the factories on piece rate, where if you wanted money, you got your head down and worked. She had made good friends in the factory, friends that she still had to this day. Pushing the memories back into the far reaches of her mind she once more looked directly into her lovers' eyes, "It really did come out of the blue," she tried to gauge his reaction, none was forthcoming. "Honestly," she reiterated, almost pleading with him to believe her words, to believe that the statement was absolute. Their friendship was more, it always had been.

Always more

Always remember you are more
More than a touch
More than a feeling
More than the words
The feelings contained deep within
Fighting to be set free
What is right?
What is wrong?
Never knowing, always dreaming
Dreams to make you feel alive
Hope to keep you going
Close your eyes and think of me
Always know you are more to me

©Angie Beastall

"So," her lovers voice hardening a little "Will you answer the original question as to why?"

Looking up as the tone of his voice had hardened, doubt creeping in. Her resolve not to hurt him cracked, "because I can, because I've always been able to do what I want, without hesitation or forethought about consequences of my words or actions!" she answered sharply, instantly regretting her outburst as the shock and hurt registered on his face. "I'm sorry," she moved from her chair to squat besides his, "Look at me," she quietly demanded. Turning his head their faces inches from each other, reaching up she gently placed the palm of her hand on his cheek, staring deeply into his eyes, trying to reach his soul, "I love you, that will never change, no matter what," leaning forward she lightly kissed him, "do you believe me?" she questioned as she pulled away, the smallest movement of his head affirmed his answer. A small smile appeared on her lips as she stood and retook her seat.

"Do I know him?" he questioned.

"Fuck, fuck, fuck," that was the one question she didn't want him to ask, if she answered truthfully, he would then realise that the third man worked with them, and that was something she didn't want him to know. A dilemma faced her, if she answered no, as she knew she must, that one lie, no matter how small would lead to another, then another. But at this moment in time the consequences of her lover knowing the identity of the third man outweighed the telling one little lie, didn't it?

Her mind questioning her actions. "No," she replied with as much conviction as she could muster, she would deal with the fallout from the lie when or if it arose.

"Where did you meet him?" he further questioned

"He's an ex-boyfriend" lie number two rolled off her tongue with ease. She had recently been on a night out with friends and had bumped into the third man, accidently on purpose. Since then, they had secretly been meeting early morning before the workday started, his kisses, his touch had ignited something in her that she had never felt before. The intensity, their intensity together was addictive. She felt the flush rising on her face at the thought of his face buried in her neck, biting down leaving his mark on her, and she in turn savaging his neck and back with her nails.

"Who started it?" he questioned further

"He did," she replied. Even after their exchanges had started, she still thought of him as a colleague who she liked to flirt with, and then the tone of his messages changed, and she instinctively knew he was asking something else.

"What did he message?"

"Well," she smiled more to herself. "The first message read I'm completely fucked" looking across at her lover she saw the confusion on his face

"He likes a drink or two or ten," she openly laughed. "Sorry," she apologised "I'm laughing at the message, not the situation."

"Does that make it any better," the hurt clear to hear.

Looking across at him, "I'm not apologising again!"

Seeing the hurt that was peeking through her lovers' façade her voice softened as she continued, "I missed you, I missed us," tears threatened once more. Bringing her hands up to her face she closed her eyes and ran the index finger from each hand across them to stop the tears from dropping onto her cheeks. "After I had opened my heart to you, you disappeared, we disappeared," she stopped, her lips trembling tears replacing her laughter, streaking her weary face. "I wrote the words to you in short stories, in the poems I sent," her voice breaking, "you ignored them, you ignored them all," the pain once more threatening to envelope her.

Hidden

Words on the page getting shorter
Feelings running deep
The touch on the skin getting less
Aching for a lovers' kiss
Meeting at the crossroads to decide
Which way to go?
The stronger the feeling
The harder the fall
Escaping to a forgotten place
Breathing in a different time
Behind the blackened windows
Forever to be hidden from view
Passions curbed, always denied
Unable to see the light of freedom
In a fleeting moment

©Angie Beastall

He reached across taking her hand, "Sorry," it was his turn to apologise, the anger stripped from his tone at the realisation of what he had done to her. And in turn what she had done to him.

Looking up, she wearily replied, "There are no words for the pain I felt, I think it made it worse because I had shared parts of my childhood with you that I have never told anyone, not even my husband." Raising her hands, she put the palms over her eyes and tilted her head back to stop the flow of even more tears. She breathed, deep long and hard, calm she told herself, calm. "Shall we have another drink?" her lover asked concern in his voice. Removing her hands "Yes," her simple reply.

Taking her phone out of her pocket she handed him the loyalty card to get stamped. The coffee shop they frequented ran a loyalty scheme where you got your card stamped nine times to get a tenth drink free. Putting the phone down next to their empties, she watched her lover walk to the counter, she knew he would be a while as a queue had formed. Tiredness washed over her, leaning forward she placed her elbows on her knees, covering her face with her hands she proceeded to rub her forehead with her fingertips. It was a compulsion for when she was upset, it calmed her. Moving her hands further down her face she circled her eyes with the middle fingers, gently massaging them. Breathing deep she counted to ten as she exhaled. The third man invading her thoughts, the memory of his lips on hers, of his hand circling her neck as he told her what he was going to do to her, her legs had buckled not only from the passion but to stop him from leaving his mark on her neck. Not that it helped she was still marked, even now. Subconsciously she lifted the collar on her work shirt to hide the evidence. A gentle smile played on her lips brightening her features as she though it was a good job that they were in the middle of a pandemic, it meant she could wear a snood around her neck, chin, and lips, making everyone none the wiser. An arm moved across her vision bringing her out of her preoccupation with the third man.

"Earth to Fi," her lover said as he placed the tray holding their second round of drinks on the table. Looking up she smiled gently at him. "You were gone then," he quizzed her, "anywhere nice?"

"Sorry," another apology followed by a gentle laugh, "I wasn't anywhere special." It was true she hadn't been anywhere special; the third man wasn't special; he was more of a compulsion. The third man had filled a void that her lover had left, she questioned whether she would have allowed him to enter her life if her lover had not rejected her love. It was a moot point, the third man was here, but only for a fleeting moment of time. Blink once he would blur, blink twice and he would be gone.

"I got you a large hot soya latte this time, is that OK?" her lover asking as he placed the drinks on the table and once more moved the empty tray to one side.

"That's fine, I meant to ask you to get me a hot drink but," she shrugged her shoulders and lifted her hands to indicate the situation. Leaning forward she picked up the warm drink and cradled it in her hands, using it like a hot water bottle, she lowered her eyes to watch the steam gently rising from her cup. Pursing her lips, she gently blew on the hot beverage before taking a precautionary sip to see if it was cool enough to drink. Closing her eyes as she took another sip, she relished the flavour and warmth of the drink before once more opening her eyes to look directly into those of her lover. "Thank you Fi," a quiet calm had descended on her. Her Fi, the warmth she felt in her heart for him was overwhelming, she knew he was real, they were real, Fi was real. The third man wasn't real she knew that, but that didn't stop her from wanting him.

She loved that they were what they called "Fi", she smiled remembering how it came about. They had been having their usual "text date" and he had said something meaningful, that had touched something within her:

"Memories fade, but the scars still linger," he had written.

"That's a bit deep."

"It's from a song I've just been listening to."

"A question has just popped into my head," she had returned

"Ask: if it is for me."

"It is for you," she had replied, "OK daft question: If you could, would you marry me? It popped into my head because I've just been eating some love hearts and one said Marry Me… I instantly though of you."

"I do think about it, but to be honest I stop as soon as the thought enters my head because you won't get divorced. However, I think I would marry you. Would you want to marry me?"

"I would," her reply genuine. "But as you state I won't get divorced. Shall we get married in another dimension that only we live in?" she hoped he was smiling when he had read her reply

"P.S." she continued, "it means a lot to me when you take into consideration that I know how you feel about marriage."

"You have awoken something in me. Perhaps we will marry when we are old and survivors."

She smiled to herself as she read his reply, "I'm tired now, it's been a long day we'll chat tomorrow…over coffee?" she asked.

"Always," the short reply

Closing her eyes she fell asleep dreaming of what ifs, buts and maybes, lost in a different dimension.

Embrace the Night

As another day draws to a close
The sun fights the onset of night with a fiery burst
A sky ablaze with the rich colour of days end
Turn your face to the dying light
Bathing in the final rays of warmth
A silent dreamscape floating in time
Waiting
Always waiting
For the dark to reign from its shadowy throne
The time for fear is past
Embrace the hope
Feel the love
Turn your face to the starry night
Close your eyes and make a wish

©Angie Beastall

"You're gone again," a voice broke through the memory at the forefront of her mind. Looking around she gazed at her lover, her Fi. "Sorry," she laughed, "I seem to spend my life apologising for one thing or another," the laugh continued, "I was gone again, wasn't I?" she questioned him the spark reaching her eyes.

"Yes," his simple reply, "Where were you this time?"

"In a special place, filled with the only ones that matter", her voice filled with the love that she had for the man sitting in front of her, concern shadowing his features.

"Was I there?" he quizzed her.

"You were," leaning across she held out her hand towards him palm up. "You are always there Fi, you and I are one, we have transcended beyond the boundaries of jealousy, the question you posed early about the third man only matters if it destroys us, and I would never allow that to happen."

She watched him lean across to take hold of her hand, turning it over his thumb and index finger took hold of the new addition to her finger twirling it, until it sat for all the world to see. Looking down she gazed at the ring he had picked for her "I love it so much," leaning across not caring who was about or who saw, she kissed him softly on his lips and whispered gently against them, "I truly do love it Fi, almost as much as I love you."

They held each other's gaze for what seemed an eternity before she pulled away asking, "Do you really need to know about me and the third man, or who the third man is?"

"I think I know who he is, but I am not sure he really matters, what we share is fluid, I have to ask myself would he ever reach our status?"

"No," conviction in her reply, "it doesn't matter, he doesn't matter, behind his façade lies a true narcissist"

"We all have a little narcissism within us, sometimes you say things that make me want to know more, to ask a barrage of questions. But you will tell me what you wish to tell me when you are ready."

She smiled at his statement, "you can ask all the questions you want to, now whether I chose to answer is the thing."

"That," he openly laughed, "is the perfect answer. I do however have a suspect in mind."

"Really" her interest peaked "tell me your suspect's name?"

"I won't tell you his name, but I will state the following: my suspect drinks in a certain bar, drinks a copious amount of alcohol and wears tortoise shell glasses. But that could be a lot of people around here and if we mutually know them then the field is narrowed! .... So," he continued "who is my suspect?"

Tortoise shell shades

Girl in the sunshine wearing the tortoise shell shades
What is happening behind the dark lenses?
The windows to your soul hidden from view
Shadows behind the shell, unknowing, unfeeling
What brings the smile to your lips?
Thoughts of a kiss?
Thoughts of a touch?
Images of a tortoise shell boy?
Girl in the tortoise shell shades smiles just for you
©Angie Beastall

"Clever," she responded, "I see what you did there, and my response is to say, if you tell me I will say yes if you are correct."

She wanted him to know, it pained her that she was keeping this from him. To keep the full extent of what had been happening between her and the third man over the last couple of months. They hadn't been intimate, she knew they never would be, but there was something that he possessed that she wanted, a strength that she needed to test. Was it the third man's strength or her strength that needed testing? That was indeed the question posed!

Her lovers voice once again poked through the fog in her mind, "You need to remember some things," his words softly spoken. "We are Fi, that means a lot to me. I know you; I am not your husband; I don't need the protection that you give him. Pain is raw material for me. Don't be afraid to hurt me, I'll consume it, I will get over the pain." Leaning towards her he gently ran his fingers slowly down her cheek, following the lines that the tears had left. "You are my Fi, you are and always will be free, but most importantly I will always forgive you," he leaned across and kissed her, pulling away his gaze never leaving hers. "You know what," he said not really asking a question, "now that you make that offer, I don't think I want confirmation: What if I'm right?" it was a question he posed more to himself than directly at her, "I need to think about that? I may ask at another time," leaning back in the small leather tub chair before continuing, "today is for us we have hurt each other enough for one day, most of the time the ticking in my head is silent, I like it that way. I love you Fi, that is all that matters."

"Shut the ticking down, it doesn't matter, he doesn't matter, he has never truly mattered, interlopers never do, that is their existence, they live in a fake world surrounded by fake hopes and desires," looking down at her hands a thought entering her head bringing a smile to her features, "he is just a story waiting to be written."

Never to be Once Upon a Time

Once upon a time isn't how the story begins
There's an answer to find on a mysterious journey
Seeking a destination yet to be revealed
Blindly jumping down the rabbit hole
Searching for the truth seen in the looking glass
A reflection of me is all I can see
Unable to run from what's in my head
Yesterday I was a different me
Powerless to stop the metamorphosis ahead
Is it madness to search for forever?
For how long can it be?
Requesting a ticket to the dark side of wonderland
For the third man and me

©Angie Beastall

Book Two

SHE

A Story of Desire

Cover my eyes with silk
I do not fear the dark
Hands bound in prayer
Unable to reach out
Plant kisses in secret places
To heighten the pleasure
Never knowing
Always wanton
Anticipation of an action
Reaction of a touch
Desire building
Desire for the touch
Desire for a caress
Desire for the dark

©Angie Beastall

The End is a state of mind

"I'm going to break you," he told her, the steel clearly heard in his voice. It sent a small shiver down her spine.

"I trust you," her reply spoken softly. It was strange, she did trust him, she knew she mustn't, but she did.

Grabbing her by the chin, he bought his face closer to hers. "Did I tell you that you could speak cunt," not really a question more of an order, "you know what happens when you speak out of turn,"...his eyes suddenly ablaze with desire and excitement.

Her stomach knotted and sparks of wanton desire crept down to her groin; "fuck" she thought "I've never wanted someone as much as I want him". He was dangerous, she knew that but didn't care, dangerous and destructive. He could not only end her, he could end her life as she knew it, but at this moment in time she only wanted him. Regrets were for later not for the here and now! She had never regretted anything that had happened in her life, after all her journey both good and bad had made her into who she was today, it had also placed her on the path that she was currently walking down.

"Just fuck me already," she replied insolence coating every word she had just spoken.

Suddenly she found herself facedown, his breathe in her ear, "what part of I am the Master, and you are the slave do you not understand? Your punishment is my reward you cum slut."...dragging her over his lap, his hand reached down pulling her panties down her legs, the Master proceeded to spank her...hard. Tears sprang instantly into her eyes, she tensed trying to block out the pain. He laughed, a long throaty deep hard laugh. "You belong to me, you always have, you just didn't know it until now. The punishment is mine to give and yours to take, and afterwards you will thank me, you will always thank me."

"How the hell had she got herself into this situation" the thought ran through her mind as the spanks intensified.

They stopped as quickly as they had started but she was still laid across his knee, one hand in the small of her back, the other gently rubbing her stinging red arse. His hand moved down and parted her thighs, "let's see how much you really enjoyed your punishment" he growled as his hand slid between her thighs cupping her now throbbing pussy. He slid two fingers in, "well, well slave, it appears that you really did enjoy your punishment, what do you say?" a hint of tenderness entering his voice as he lightly landed a single spank on her derriere.

"Thank you."

A harder spank landed. "Thank you what?"

"Thank you for my punishment, Master."

"You will learn to love your punishment, after all a slave's role is to pleasure her Master and my pleasure is your pain."

What do you see?

Tell me what you see deep in my eyes
As we sit face to face
Do you feel our souls merge?
Waiting for the right time and place
Transport me to where we can be free
Where the shackles of life are gone
There are no boundaries here to see
Only you
Only me
Only us
M/s

©Angie Beastall

She thought back to the beginning of her journey and the innocent banter that she had exchanged with the third man. He had been an enigma to her, she knew that she needed to explore the puzzle that was the third man. A question arose within her mind; would she still go down the rabbit hole if she had known where the journey would lead?

A simple enough question. It deserved a straight-forward answer.

Yes, came the instantaneous reply. She would jump down the rabbit hole even if she had known where it would land her. She wanted something from him, something that he could never know she wanted. And when she had it, she would take it and run. But for now, she would play his game.

She would lull him into thinking that he would soon control every aspect of her life, well when she was on her "own" anyway, she still belonged to him 24/7 as he was her Master, but her homelife was just that, hers. During the questioning phase prior to when the Total Power Exchange (TPE for short} would come into play she had asked about limitations and the fact that she was married was a major limitation. Game or not, she never thought that she would allow someone to have so much control over her after going through the sexual, physical and emotional abuse of her childhood, but his force of personality was strong and her attraction to him was overwhelming, she would need to tread very carefully before she found herself falling for him, if she did, she would be unable to resist him. This was a journey she needed to take, she would do anything and become whomever he desired her to be just to be with him.

Maybe the strong attraction she felt for him was because of the systematic abuse that she had suffered for most of her childhood. It had certainly been drilled into her that during these dark times that she must always do as she was told, and that "Daddy" was the only one that loved her, and his special love was the only way of showing her how much he loved her. Stupid, stupid child she had scolded herself countless times for being so dumb, but when you are only six and know nothing else, the adults are always right, and Daddy's love was the normal in her life. Not that she saw her would be Master as the Daddy, she thought him stronger than that, stronger than her. A test she had to remind herself.

Would get from him what she needed? Craved even. But she did have to question just what it was exactly that she wanted from him? Now that really is the question?

She pondered on the men currently in her life:

Her Husband

Her Lover

The Third Man, who she would allow to be Her Master

Her life certainly was full, she laughed to herself, it wasn't really a laughing at a joke laugh, it was more maniacal, she was spiralling out of control, after all this was revenge, wasn't it? And didn't they say that revenge was best served cold? Her current state was extremely far from cold, it was more like a lava flow. That thought bought a small smile to her lips, this was revenge of a different nature, it would take going down into the dark recesses of her mind to a place where what she called "The Child" lived.

The Child was her hurt, her pain, her guilt, her anguish. Most of all The Child was her lost childhood, it was the laughter that never was, the candyfloss never eaten, the friendless days and the long nights listening to the deafening sound of silence, but mostly it was the anger. The anger of innocence lost. Tears sprang immediately to her eyes at the thought of "The Child" that she tried so hard to keep locked up, but emotional turmoil always unwittingly unlocked the door where The Child lived. The Child had briefly surfaced last year when she had fallen in love, a deep unforgiving love that had consumed her very soul, the love had not been reciprocated and this had taken its toll on her emotions. She had laced up her trainers and taken to the pavements, running towards the dawn, towards an answer, the argument rising in her mind, the miles felt endless until The Child had eventually return to the dark.

Breaking Dawn

A new day had begun
Running towards the breaking dawn
A crossroads reached, reflect, decide
Eyes glistening, tears streaking her face
Her mind in turmoil
An emotional crisis to fight
Screaming for the pain to stop
Is she strong enough?
A question asked, an answer to find
The strength of armour stripped bare
Only fragility left, an open wound
Running towards the dawn
Always running
One step at a time
One thought at a time

©Angie Beastall

She didn't want or need to dwell on the past, always look forward. Her past was exactly that, her past. Well, now it was. It had been the argument in her mind with The Child and the countless miles she had ran for her to realise just how strong she really was, an epiphany had hit as her feet pounded on the ground, whilst the music played in her ear, she had posted it on her social media page, it was something that she wouldn't usually post as it would make her look like a nutjob, but the feeling and emotion had been so strong

Epiphany…

Now there's a word you don't drop every day…

It has taken me 51 years 3 months and 14 days to get mine, I know what you're thinking "religious nut" …NO. The other one:

A realisation:

Just me, a sunrise, running shoes, stunning scenery, and music…relaxing, putting one foot in front of the other:

Pounding

Always Pounding…. Onward

A thought

A feeling

What am I?

Who am I?

Where had that come from?

I am a daughter, a sister, a wife, a lover, a confidant, a friend, a foe, a stranger

I am a factory lass, an office worker, a postie.

Like scrooge we all have ghosts. Ghosts of the past. Ghosts of the present. Fear of the future yet to be written. The path taken and the people we meet help mould and shape who we are for the future.

We love, laugh, cry, and feel. In the pandemic world of today, touch is limited so use your other senses: See, Hear, Taste and Smell.

See the good in people, listen to advise offered, Grab the Taste for adventure, Smell out the bullshit of liars.

'I am who I have met.

I will be who I am yet to meet.

But most of all I am finally me.'

So, here she was just about to add to the list:

A slave.

But what was it exactly that she was adding, was it an adventure? A calling? A need? She didn't know but she knew she had to find out. The rabbit hole was beckoning, and the calling was strong.

She thought back to the recent conversation she had had with her now "Master".

"You do understand it's not a game, don't you?" he had asked. His stark blue eyes boring into hers, his face close enough for her to see the tiredness around his eyes, the tiredness the product of his lifestyle. She tried not to worry about him, but she always had, it was in her nature to. She liked to think that first and foremost he was her friend, but sometimes even that was uncertain.

He towered above her, being six feet to her tiny five foot two. This wasn't really an issue to her; after all her husband was well over six foot tall. It was his personality that scared her sometimes, he was an angry person, she wasn't sure who or what made him angry. She had once said to him "life's too short to be that angry all the time" his short staccato reply, "It has served me well" …

"Yes, I do understand it's not a game," she had replied her mind thinking about what she couldn't really voice, after all revenge has never been a game, continuing she asked, "you need to tell me your full expectations."

"I expect you to belong to me, I expect you to be obedient, compliant and committed to your Master."

A strange feeling rose within her at the thought of belonging to him, God knows why, after all her independence was part of her, but in her mind, she would only belong to him when she was on her own. He couldn't control every aspect of her life, after all she was married and her strength, her will wouldn't or more importantly couldn't allow full control. She could make him think that he was in control, manipulation really did come easy to her, she was a chameleon, being able to change to fit into whatever situation she found herself in. She had learnt at an early age that it hurt less if you were compliant, or at least appeared to be.

"You have my full commitment."

"Are you sure," he questioned, "I would love to own a slave fully again?"

"One hundred per-cent sure."

"I'm glad," a smile playing around his lips his eyes lighting up, "I want to mould you and turn you into my slave, my cum slut."

"Me too Fucker, me too"

A serious note crept into his voice, "Do you really want it?"

"Yes Fucker, I like the thought of you owning me."

"Me too, so fucking much." His hand came up gripping her neck, his lips barely touching hers. She breathed him in, she loved the smell of him, his aftershave mixed with his strength of personality, along with the promise of brutality. "You won't be calling me Fucker for much longer you know."

"I know," she answered him, her eyes closing, breathing deep once more, drinking him in, his aroma, his strength, but also his vulnerability, "but whilst I can, I will." Her eyes opening, the mischief playing in them clear to see crept down to her lips, a small smile appearing.

His stare burned into her, before moving down to look at the small smile playing on her lips, his grip on her neck tightened. "If you mean what you say and have no problem with me seeing other people?" he questioned.

"I have no issues at all, after all your time is your own, as is mine"

What she couldn't say was after all I have a husband that you know about and a lover that you don't. Her lover was the only person that truly knew her, well, as well as anyone could know her, after all she only allowed them to see and know what she wanted them to. Her relationship with her lover was fluid, no expectations, they just were! She didn't really know her, after all if she did why would she willingly put herself on what could be a path of destruction?

For what? Revenge? Need? Belonging? A story?

All of you

All is lost when I look in your eyes
Dreams fill my mind of things that cannot be
Place your hand gently on my cheek
Pull me close
Loose yourself in this moment
Tell me of you
Show me of you
Give me all of you
Falling, falling…. too fast to stop
My eyes see only you
My heart feels only you
My lips taste only you
What of sense?
What of need?
What of danger?
Only us, only we exist
M/s

Sense, need, danger. They were all too real, need was the most dangerous, her need to feel him, to belong to him may outweigh her need to have her revenge on him.

She thought back to when he was the third man, a nickname entailed to him by her when talking about him with her Lover. The third man was just a visitor in her life where the visitors pass could be declined at any moment. It had taken a lot for her to decide to terminate his pass. He was an alcoholic and alcohol is a mistress best served wet and cold. And she was warm, or at least she liked to think she was. She couldn't compete with this mistress on a normal level, but maybe she could compete with it on a darker more animalistic level, or she hoped she could. She was selfish she admitted that much about herself, but did selfish make her cold? She had once told The Third Man that he needed to have a thirst for something else, and when he had asked "A thirst for what" her reply was simple "Me" she stated simply "you need to have a thirst for me". She really hadn't liked that he had systematically refused to meet her and cancelled their clandestine meetings without a moment's notice. How dare he! her anger rose, just who the fuck did he think he was? She needed to keep the rejection, the hurt and the anger alive, it would keep her on the path she had chosen, after all it was a story that needed to be told.

Would it be her redemption?

Could it be her downfall?

Opposites

Reflect on the stillness showing
Turmoil hidden

Peace and calm reign above
Uncertainty below

Mirrored clouds soft and free
Storm's building

Absorb the tranquillity of nature
Exude confusion

©Angie Beastall

ab initio

"How far along this path do you want to go," he inquired?

"Always to the end."

"That's excellent. But even though this is somewhat extreme, you are sure?"

"I am sure, it's going to be a huge learning curve, I have a couple of questions," her voice held uncertainty.

"Go on," his voice held a cautionary note.

"It will be only you and me, won't it?"

"Yes," he replied "It will only be you and I."

"I have been reading up about various things online, would you like me to have a day collar?"

Again, an affirmative was uttered from his lips

"Is the collar of your choice?" she enquired further. She needed to know as much as possible before she managed to get herself into a hole that she may not be able to escape from.

"Of course," he replied, "they don't come off either."

"OK" she confirmed that she understood

"Are you happy that it is just us?" he fired a question back.

"I am happy that it is just us." After all it would make it harder for her to do what she needed to do if there were others involved.

"Do you buy the collar?" she quizzed him.

"Indeed, I do."

"New year present for me then," she replied laughing.

"Yes," his voice serious, "Have a look and see what your limits are size wise and show me."

"I was looking on the internet last night." Taking her phone out of her pocket she showed him the screen shot of the necklace that she liked. It looked like a nice normal necklace not quite a D-ring, it would sit just below the throat. To the outside world it would look like a nice plain necklace, but in the BDSM world it would show that she was owned by a Master.

"I would also like a tattoo, obviously a discrete one," she continued, not knowing why she wanted one, but it was something she needed to do, more for her than for him.

"Really?" he questioned, "my ex had one, if this goes where I want it to go then yes, I will allow you to have a tattoo."

She suddenly felt a little apprehensive, she lowered my head so as not to show him.

"What," he said putting his hand under her chin and lifting her head back up so he could see into her eyes as he probed further. "What's wrong?"

"If I'm being truthful, I have a feeling of dread in case I disappoint you."

"Disappoint how." Confusion appearing on his face.

"By not being good enough I suppose?" her voice barely a whisper.

"How not good enough?" the confusion turning to concern.

"I don't know?" The truth be told she didn't, but that was The Child creeping into the equation and whenever The Child appears sorrow usually wasn't far behind.

Her emotions were currently all over the place, on one hand the plan was for revenge, but on the other she still didn't want to disappoint the man standing in front of her. The man that was staring intently into her eyes, the man that was soon to be her Master.

"You must know," a little anger now tinged his voice.

"I suppose there is no right and wrong…. Only pleasure and pain!"

"Then why say it?" his voice held a note of anger, "Hopefully there will be lots of both pleasure and pain," the anger fading as quickly as it had risen.

Side stepping the issue she had created, she posed another question

"Was your ex's tattoo of your choice and design?"

"It was my choice, yes, it was a slave register barcode."

"I saw some barcodes online, is there really a slave register?"

"There is indeed."

"Is your ex still registered as your slave?"

"Not any longer, no."

"Do we need to have a discussion about Do's and Don'ts before the TPE kicks in?" she continued.

Looking straight at her, he replied slowly as he reached across and ran his fingertips down her face. "As I have said you have until the first of January to ask away, after that you will belong to me."

"So, I wouldn't be able to ask you my usual random questions that pop into my head on a daily basis?"

"As long as you ask properly."

"Is there a correct way to ask?" #CONFUSED was an understatement, "because I do send a message saying Question? Now and usually don't ask until you reply…Is that incorrect?"

"No, that's fine."

"All good then fucker aren't we," she laughed deep, the sparkle showing in her blue eyes

"Yes, I suppose we are."

"Have you been thinking much about it?" he probed.

"All the time," she could feel the blush rising, the warmth filling her face. She liked to think herself to be a woman of the world but was amazed that sometimes she could still get embarrassed in certain situations.

"Good, I want it in your mind constantly, no matter where you are."

"It is."

"Really," It wasn't a question. The pleasure could clearly be heard in his voice at the admission, "And it will stay that way."

Only You

The touch of your mouth
The feel of your tongue
Your hands on my face, drawing me in
Your hands on my neck, holding me steady
Your hands on my body, setting it alight
Kiss me deep
Kiss me long
My mind in turmoil, my body on fire
The pain, the hurt, the pleasure

©Angie Beastall

*****

Christmas would soon be here, she was ready for the break, work had been hectic, but hectic these days was the new norm. It had been crazy busy since the pandemic had hit, and the world at large were suddenly afraid to venture past their front doors. The new going to the shops was browsing online and hitting the "checkout" button.

She was going away for a couple of days with her husband, they had a good relationship and sex life, now. Their sex life had been a little stunted, and for a few years she hadn't been interested in it at all, it had taken meeting her lover and having a frank conversation about her childhood that had set her mind asking if she was somehow punishing her husband for the sins of the father! To her, liking sex always held guilt, guilt at the enjoyment she got out of it. When she was younger, long before she had met and married her husband, she had had numerous sexual partners, far too many to remember, some didn't even have names, it was "just sex".

She often wondered why her husband wasn't enough. But his tastes weren't the same as hers, well not in the bedroom anyway. She had learnt a little about the BSDM world when she had met an older man four years into her marriage. The attraction they had for each other was strong and she couldn't help herself, and so "The Affair" started. The Affair had slowly introduced things to her that the strait-laced community would class as debased. She didn't care what the outside world thought about it, she loved it and that was all that mattered. The sensation of the candle wax being dropped on her body, the intensity of the split second of heat on her naked skin before it cooled, his fresh breath blowing on her molten skin. Even thinking about it sent her mind and body into overdrive, goosebumps appearing on her skin, her nipples hardening as though begging for the wax to return.

Rimming popped into her mind, or if you want to use the posh term Analingus, it was a practice that she and The Affair had partaken of on a weekly basis. Having both given it and received it, she preferred to receive it, but what she and The Affair had was a mutual trust affair where give and take was the nature.

So, she hadn't really been shocked or surprised when a recent conversation with her soon to be Master had broached this very subject.

"So" she had enquired "besides humiliation, medical play and golden showers is there anything else I should know about?"

"Bondage, CP, Rimming and obedience training," came the short but not shocking reply.

"Rimming as in Bum Hole"? she knew exactly what rimming was, fuck knows why she had asked for clarification!

"Indeed."

"Who is rimming who?"

"You are."

"I'm rimming you?"

"Yes, it's what a slave does."

Oh well the single thought in her head he must know at some point I'm not a plain jane when it comes to sex, "It's been a while! do you enjoy it?" she replied casually.

"Very much," came the short reply.

"Do you also give it?" she questioned; metaphoric fingers crossed in her head

"Do you like it?"

"I do."

"Then yes, I do give it."

"As a reward?"

"Yes."

"I'm glad."

She was incredibly pleased, having once again found herself a playmate who liked to play in the same arena as her. Albeit a darker arena than she was used to, but new experiences excited her and the thought of being "opened" up by him made her very horny indeed.

This journey to the dark side of wonderland had started with a random statement she had said to him, knowing what she needed to do to pique his interest, to once more open the dialogue between them.

"I would like you to use everything on me that is in your drawer."

"I see, and what do you think is in my drawer?" his expression as cold as the concrete he adored

"From what you have previously stated, Rope, candle, wand and bondage tape."

"Ahhhhh," his finger tapping against his lip, "Now I recall," a smile appearing on his lips, that didn't quite reach his eyes.

"Is there more that needs adding to the list?" she asked, reading into the Ahhhhh there was more in the drawer than what he had previously mentioned.

"There is far more in the drawer, there always was."

"Are you willing to tell me?"

"I don't know if I should," he simply stated, "there is some heavy stuff in there."

"Well, in your words Just tell me?" she really wanted to know.

"Nipple clamps, pumps, vacuum pump, labia clamps, dildos, butt plugs, speculums etc.... Happy?"

"Extremely, what exactly are the pumps for, how big is the butt plug and does it vibrate?"

"Pumps for nipples, clit, pussy, various butt plugs small to large, but none vibrate."

"Very interesting." She was more than interested she was fascinated; she really did want to play. So, she asked, "Question?"

"Go on," he stated

"Do you want to play?" it was out in the open. It could only go one of two ways yes or no; it was that simple.

"Play?" he sounded bemused.

"Play, you know I want you and I want you to introduce me into your world."

"You want all of those then?" a spark appearing in his stark blue eyes.

"Would I ask otherwise?"

The question she asked hung in the air, his brow furrowed, leaning forward he brushed a stray hair away from her face before moving his hand down, to grip her neck once again.

"This isn't a game, if you want this you need to know how serious I am."

"I'm not going to know that without doing it am I?"

"No but be aware I don't fuck about with this. A slave really is a slave. A fuckhole, cumslut etc…"

"I get that!" she retorted

"You had better get it." He replied as his hand gripped tighter with each syllable uttered, the adrenaline pulsing through her veins.

'What have I done?' the question screaming in her head, choosing to ignore it she continued "I want to belong to you, I want you to own me, I want you to own all of me." She closed her eyes and lowered her head slightly, the grip he had on her neck loosened slightly.

"Look at me," he demanded," that is a strong statement to make."

She opened her eyes, his bright blue eyes cutting straight into her. His stare hard, like an icy hand reaching into her soul. She loved his eyes, they were bottomless, icy and cold, she had never seen a blue like it, the nearest blue to them she had seen was a pool of water at the bottom of Snowdon in Wales. The blue was startling, it was bright because the water was also poisonous.

His eyes may have been cold, but his gaze held the promise of his words and actions, "I believe you do," his head lowered as his lips captured hers.

He drew away his gaze never leaving hers. "I know it is a strong statement and I mean it one hundred percent," she whispered against his moist lips

"I truly hope you do." He replied as his hand moved around her neck, his fingers lightly digging into the nape of her neck "I really do want this."

"As do I, so very much." Moving her head back slightly to feel his hand grip her neck tighter.

"So very much eh!" a playful tone entering his voice.

"Obviously."

"Why obviously?" he questioned.

"Because it's you," there were no more words forthcoming as it was an instinct, a deep routed instinct that turned her into something that she wasn't… he turned her meek.

"Do you have any concerns?" he questioned.

"No, why do ask about concerns?" her brow furrowing.

"Because you need to be sure."

"I'm the surest I've been about anything…. Ever," she replied. "Even I'm surprised by how sure I am… you will be my Master and I will be your slave."

"And why are you so sure?" he quizzed her further.

"Because I want to feel that I truly belong, to close my mouth and open my mind."

"I like that," a smile playing on his lips.

"Truth is always good, isn't it?"

Truth, she thought to herself, what is truth? Had she ever really been truthful even to herself? Inwardly she was squirming, the impact that her small statement had caused in her mind raised numerous questions. She needed to explore aspects of her personality that she knew were part of her, they were the parts that she didn't like. Was she getting into this to punish herself? Or to even destroy herself?

Why would she need to do either? After all wasn't it about revenge?

Her mask was slipping, she could feel it. She had always said, "we all wear masks the only difference is some deny that they are wearing them."

What mask did she wear?

What mask did he wear?

Her brain went into overdrive thinking about the question posed... his mask was easy to figure out, it was anger or that was her opinion anyway, a mask of anger to hide the vulnerability, we were all vulnerable at some level, the only thing was admitting to it, to which human nature wouldn't allow us to. She supposed her mask was a show of strength, all her vulnerability has been stripped bare at an early age, there was nothing that could happen to her that hadn't happened already. She often thought she was still that child stood naked in the living room sobbing, the anguish, the despair, the vulnerability, all hidden and locked away. She swore when she ran away from home at fifteen that she would never allow herself to be defenceless again. Yet here she was... defenceless!

Masks

Work is like a glass partition
I can see, but unable to touch.
Home is for the wearing of masks
Each painted with its own expression
One for love and marriage
One for happy and sad
One for the Lover and one for the Master
Only when I am truly alone can I be me.
Time to stop, time to think
My mind sees only you, and your steely eyes of blue
Lost in the escapism of our creation
Dreaming of castles in the sky
Your arms so far away from me
I lay shattered at the feet of my own destructive path
©Angie Beastall

"Where do you want to start?" she asked.

"At the beginning of course," he laughed, at what she had no idea, probably at her naivety. She didn't really mind after all she was a novice in this world.

"What does the beginning entail?" she questioned further.

"Of the journey, we will see."

There was nothing else for her to say except for, "OK". The journey will start where it starts and ends where it ends.

"Are you sure you want this?" he questioned once more.

"Yes," she affirmed, "have you got concerns? Is that why you keep asking?"

"No, I just need you to be sure after all this will be extreme," his whole body became still. "How far are you willing to go?" he questioned further; she had never heard him so serious.

"As far as you are willing to take me," it was true, she would do as he asked without question or hesitation.

"You know how far I want to take you."

"Yes, I do, beyond the boundaries of the journeys end."

"That would be my ideal, I never thought I'd be in this position again. With someone who wanted to enter it fully…. all aspects."

Looking him squarely in the eyes. "You should never say never, it's amazing the people you meet."

"Indeed, it is, I want this to be what I said. I want you marked and owned," he smiled down at her. She smiled back. His smile this time reaching his eyes, it didn't happen very often, but when it does his whole persona changes. He truly was a man of many levels, and she wanted to explore all that he was, is and yet to be.

"When do you want this to start?"

"New year. Fresh start, don't you think?"

"I do." She returned the smile that was once more playing at the corners of his lips. It didn't stay there for very long as he once more turned serious.

"For the final time, are you sure?" he questioned.

Without hesitating, her gaze never leaving his, "Yes," was all there was left to say.

"OK, then," his head moving close to hers, "let's get my property marked up."

The End is only the beginning

The new year was drawing ever closer......

New Year New Start

The first of the year approaches
A new me, a new you
A slave for my master laid bare before him
Eyes of black, lips of red, locks of gold
Stocking feet poised
Look long, look deep
The clock strikes twelve
The path has been chosen
The exchange takes place
I am yours, collared and silent
Mould me, teach me, create me
A new year, a new start, a new us
M/s

©Angie Beastall

Book Three

!

22-842-928-983

Dark desire within grows ever stronger
The Master has declared his ownership
A contract entered and certified
The property of her Master, owned, controlled, barcoded
the slave seeks approval from The Master
Patiently waiting for an answer or an action
A gesture to show a slave's commitment to her Master
Branded and marked with his name
Eyes downcast, head bowed in penitence
He is perpetual, immutable, ineradicable
and slave is his property
The Master is: The dawn, The day, The night
Master is.....
M/s

A Question of Ego

"Are you worthy of my servitude?"

The question she asked echoed around the stark bare walls of The Masters flat. She looked around having never really noticed before how devoid of emotion the flat was. It was warm from the heat, yet cold at the same time. A barren wasteland, white walls, wooden floors, blackout blinds hung at the windows. They were down which was not unusual, they always were. She had to wonder if he was trying to keep something out, or something in?

Her mind came back to the here and now and the question she had just asked her Master, it was straightforward enough, wasn't it? Inwardly she questioned herself, the question was clear but the world she had entered wasn't. Her Master looked at her, she could usually read his expression, but this time she couldn't. Had she gone too far with this question? anxiety rising in her mind. Questioning the Masters' status was a fine line between pleasure and pain.

"Is it wrong of me to ask such a serious question?" her eyes lowered as a sign of respect to her Master waiting for him to respond with an answer or an action.

"Sit," was the only word that passed his lips, his tone strict.

Her stocking feet silently moved across the bare wooden floor to the rug that was placed in the centre of the room, lowering her body to sit on her legs, her head bowed in penitence.

sitting down beside her The Master moved his head towards hers and whispered: "Am I worthy?" the tone in his voice was monochrome, she couldn't tell if the question had displeased him.

"In my eyes Master, yes you are worthy…but in your eyes Master, I am asking if you deem that you are worthy of my servitude?" What the actual fuck! was all she could think. What the actual fuck! shut up before you dig yourself a bigger hole. But she couldn't help herself, she needed to know if he truly was stronger than her and therefore worthy of her and so the question was posed.

"I answered this previously have I not?" was all The Master said.

#Confused was an understatement, she still didn't know what to think, she was new to the whole BDSM scene, having dabbled a little in the past with the man she called "The Affair" but nothing as deep as what The Master wanted. She had searched the internet on the subject and found a few sites, but they only offered a small insight into the world of BDSM. Her main interest lay with medical play and humiliation. It not only fascinated her, but it also made her conscious and sub-conscious aware. Truthfully, it also turned her on; some of the images that others would see as brutal, she saw as pleasurable. On the few occasions that The Master had called her slut or cum-slut she had enjoyed those exchanges. But to continue with the subject on worthiness, based on the information she had read online she was under the impression that the slave also chose to serve a worthy Master…was he worthy? She didn't know, maybe his idea of worthy was different to hers, maybe that was a question for later as she felt she was treading a fine line, and the tightrope was getting thinner along with what could be his patience.

"I know what I am," his voice strong but quiet, "I am asking slave who obviously doesn't know."

"Enlighten me Master, please?"

"Enlighten you how slave?"

"By telling me what you are."

She wanted him to tell her straight, she was an independent woman, she always had been. But this man, her Master, had done something no other person could do, he had taken control of her soul, it scared her, the control he had over her. As she continued to sit waiting for a response from her Master, she thought back to the conversation they had had a few days earlier.

"I feel like I have a dual personality now, her and slave." Master had laughed as had she. "I believe the slave is winning though," she had told him. This pleased him greatly as the smile reached his eyes.

"The slave will win out; nothing is more important," the seriousness that had entered his tone made her look intently at him.

"I know Master, my role is to please you, nothing else matters now."

"And do you genuinely mean that slave? Nothing else?"

"I believe I do, to be perfectly truthful, it scares me a little, but it excites me more Master."

His brow furrowed, "why does it scare you slave?"

"Because it makes me vulnerable, and I swore I would never go there again. I trust you Master. I have entered this of my own volition and therein lies the difference. My feelings for you are very strong and quite possibly dangerous Master."

"Why do you think dangerous?"

" Not physically dangerous Master."

"I know slave, so why?"

"Because it could end something else Master."

"What could it end slave?" he probed further. She really didn't want to say, she could have kicked herself for opening this particular can of worms. She hesitated, taking a deep breathe before she continued, "It could if I allowed it end what I have with my husband, so that world needs to be kept separate from ours. Ours is just us, The Master and his slave."

"And why could it end that?"

He really wasn't going to let this one lie she thought… bollocks! "That would depend on The Masters marks… Master"

"Explain please?"

"If you leave any bruises, I'm not a nun Master and I sleep in the buff."

"But I will leave marks slave, so perhaps you need to re-think if you don't want it to end with him."

"I have never had any doubts that you would leave your mark on me Master, I do not need to re-think I will deal with the marks. My fate was sealed the day you sent me your first message, besides I have had ten years of practice covering up marks."

"Is that right," he queried "about your fate being sealed?"

"Absolutely Master."

"And why was that?"

"Because it's you Master," she answered truthfully. Her feelings were usually locked up tightly inside, hardly ever seeing the light of day. But, her Master was disarming, she didn't know why he had the effect he did on her, all she knew was that he completed her.

"Aren't you worried it could end what you have?"

He really wasn't going to let this one go, she thought.

"I am and always have been a selfish fucker, it's all about me, well technically it's about you, My Master, your expectations for me will never change." She looked at a spec of fluff on the floor as she spoke

"Look at me slave" The Master demanded "Repeat my expectations"

"You expect me to belong to you, you expect me to be obedient, compliant and committed to you Master."

"Good, but you still haven't answered my question slave."

"I am afraid it will end what I have, but I've spent forty years hiding, I don't want to do it anymore. I want to be free to be me. Any consequences that arise are mine to deal with Master."

"You think it will end what you have genuinely?" a note of concern rising.

"Genuinely, I don't know Master." Her mind going into crisis mode, the fear that this world, their world could come crashing down outweighed everything and anything else.

"It doesn't alter us does it, Master? The thought of not having him in her life made her blurt out the question before she could ask his permission.

His voice gentle as he replied, "No slave, it doesn't alter us."

"I will ask you once more," he continued, "I know you know the answer slave, I want your honesty. Does it worry you?"

His gentle side was her undoing. "If I'm truly honest with myself Master, it's not about my husband finding out, it's about me walking away from him for you….and that is what scares me Master."

There, it was out in the open, she held her breath, she didn't feel better; in fact, once more she felt her vulnerability trying to break out of the dark place of her mind. His voice snapped her out of it.

"And you think that as you get deeper and become real property that is how you may feel?"

"I don't know, Master, it will be what it will be, won't it?"

"It will slave yes."

"Master," she bowed her head once more. She didn't want him to see the raw that she knew was in her eyes.

"Let's hope it doesn't come to that for you slave."

"I came into this forewarned" she continued. "I have always known where your proclivities lie." She raised her head and looked him squarely in the face, she would get punished for this infraction she knew that, but a point needed to be made. His face showed shock but only for a milli-second before his normal composure returned.

"And where slave do you think they lay?" Reaching his hand across and gently running his fingertips down her cheek.

Shit, shit, shit was all that ran through her mind, maybe it was poor judgement for her to try and make a point. His hand moved further down her face until it stopped at its destination, her neck. He curled his fingers around it applying pressure.

"Well slave, if you have something to say now is the time to say it."

Back in the Room

"Is that a question?" Master clicked his fingers. "Don't make me repeat myself slave."

She zoned back into the here and now, tucking away the memory of the brutality and punishment of that day, still fresh not only in her mind but also on her body. She had displeased her Master and the punishment that she had received fitted the crime. She was never sure what punishment was fitted to any crime, she judged that it was more according to the Master's mood.

"Apologies Master for my initial lack of response, it is more of a request as demands are no longer my place."

She raised her head slightly to see the small smile playing at the corners of his lips.

"I've told you what I am before, have I not?"

"A fucker Master?" Her voice showing that she really wasn't sure.

Standing to show his full six-foot frame, The Master towered over her still prone body and bowed head, he reached down to take her hand helping her to stand. "I am Master and you are my property."

"Yes Master." … she wanted to feel his kiss, his touch, she ached for him, she wanted him, but most of all she wanted to please him, to please him would warrant his attention, and to receive his attention, no matter how slight, was her true craving.

"Are you sure?" he quizzed.

"Yes Master, hence the tattoos."

He had registered her on the Slave registry and had received the certificate of registration stating that he now owned her, the certificate came with a unique barcode and number. She had always loved tattoos, she had had her first tattoo at seventeen, and her second at thirty. Recently had a new musical tattoo of her own design, it had been part of one her sketches and as soon as she signed the piece in her trademark signature of "Fucker" in musical notes she knew instantly that she wanted it as a tattoo, so at the age of fifty-two she had had her third tattoo. Now once more she had increased her tattoo count. He hadn't demanded she have the barcode tattoo, in fact she had suggested it, not only to show him of her commitment to her Master, but because she loved not only the barcode but what it represented.

"Question Master if it pleases you?" she spoke then held her tongue. She would not ask the question until he had approved it. It showed respect for her Master, she tried to always be respectful, but it was hard, she had been independent for a very long time.

"Go on?"

"Am I respectful enough Master?"

"It does slip sometimes but it's flagged up."

"Independence takes some changing Master."

"I'm sure it does."

"Further Question Master if it pleases you?" she asked once more. She wasn't sure what her limit was on the number of questions she could ask before Master got frustrated with her.

"Go on Slave."

"The tattoos?" she didn't need to say anything further as The Master responded instantly.

"I have thought about them, and I will let you know tomorrow."

She had plans for some new ink but needed permission from her Master first and foremost.

"Apologies Master," her eyes once more cast downwards.

"Better."

"I don't mean to be a bad slave Master," closing her eyes to stop the tears that were forming, "I just want to please you, and what better way than once again declaring my servitude to you with new tattoos."

"I'm sure you don't mean to be a bad slave, but once a question is asked, I will answer in my own time."

"Am I being a twat?" she quizzed.

"I think you are," he responded, "and where's the fucking Master," he snapped.

"Apologies Master," fuck she thought I've never apologised so much in my entire life.

"So," he questioned, "Why do you think you are being a twat?"

"For asking a question you have answered previously."

He leaned towards her. "Look at me," he demanded.

She raised her head and looked straight into his eyes, once again she was lost.

"I am Master, and you are property"

"Yes Master."

"Are you sure?"

"Yes Master."

"Repeat it slave"

"You are Master, and I am property."

"I have a question for you slave," his tone serious, "you always said you were not one hundred percent sub, never mind a slave...What changed?"

"You, Master. There is nothing else to say, just you. I want you and everything that is you," she could feel the blush rising up her face.

"I see slave, so that got rid of any Dom tendency?" he quizzed further.

She looked straight at him as she replied, "probably not if I'm being totally honest, it's still there, I just need to suppress it or get punished Master."

"Good slut, hopefully I can help with that," he spoke quietly whilst one hand snaked into her hair, taking a handful to drag her face to his as his other hand circled her neck applying enough pressure for her to know his intentions. His lips pressed onto hers, his tongue invading her mouth, she kissed him back matching the harshness, winding her arms around him, her nails digging into his flesh, she would pay for that later, dearly. But she didn't care. He did things to her mind and body that she thought she would never experience in her lifetime. Lifting her from the floor she wrapped her legs around his waist, backing up he crashed her into the wall of the living room. Her head flung back as his mouth replaced his hand on her neck, biting down hard. Her mind went into overdrive, her body into ecstasy. Fuck, it didn't take much for her to want him, just his smell sent her senses into overdrive, his teeth biting into her flesh, she knew there would be a mark for her to cover, but at this moment in time, here in her Master's flat, feeling him pushing against her, his harshness, his brutality, him.... just him .... she really didn't give a fuck.

"It's time for my bath Slave," he spoke against her burning skin, "and when you've bathed me, I'm going to open you wide and tease your pee-hole with the new sounding bars you have recently presented me with."

She shivered, thoughts of that day sprang into her memory, his face had been stunned or even startled, she couldn't really make her mind up which it was, at the latest gift she had given him. "Are you pleased with them Master?" she had asked concerned if he said no.

"Yes slave, I am very pleased," he had kissed her lightly.

"You feel you want to experience that?" he had questioned "get stretched over time?"

"At your pleasure Master."

"Excellent."

"Yes Master."

 His words once more returned her back from the memories that constantly played in her mind. "But not before you've done what a good slave should do, and, if you please your Master, I shall reward you in kind."

She blushed; her body tingled at the thought of Master rimming her.

"Question Master if it pleases you?"

"Yes slave."

"Ref: rimming, just tongue or can I use fingers?" ordinarily she would never ask questions like this, but there were no barriers left between them.

"I prefer just the tongue, as deep as you can slave."

"Yes Master."

"Excellent slave, then I will examine your fuckhole, wide and deep, and tease your pee-hole."

"I'm sure you will open me wide enough to see my soul, Master."

"And then some slave, and then some," putting her down so her feet once more touched the floor he spun her around and playfully smacked her arse. "Now go and run me a bath and wait for me in the tub."

"Ad imperium tumm" a small smile played on her bruised lips, "at your command, I look forward to pleasing you, Master."

"Me too slave, me fucking too."

She loved bathing him, running her soapy hands across his body, his back to her, his head resting on her chest. She walked across the hall which was as devoid of emotion as the living room, same wooden floor running through from the living room. The bathroom visually felt a little warmer but maybe that was due to the pastel tone the walls were painted, another blackout blind at the window but this one open to let in the fresh air from the small open window. She bent down to put the plug in and turn on the hot tap. Standing she turned and silently moved across to study the one framed artwork on the wall, a naked male torso, arms crossed in front of the body, a large crucifix hung from his neck, a tattoo half showing on his upper arm. It had been printed in black and white which suited the pose...who was it she wondered?

Turning once more she bent to check the temperature of the water before turning on the cold water to mix...steam rose from the bath filling the small space. Swirling the water around to mix the cold with the hot, she felt him rather than heard him enter the bathroom. "I thought I'd told you to wait in the tub Slave," his voice echoed around the walls mixing with the sound of running water.

" It is very nearly ready for you Master."

He came up behind her and ran his fingers lightly across the barcode tattoo that ran across the top of her shoulder. "You truly are mine now slave," before bending his head and kissing it lightly.

"I'm pleased Master, I know you had your concerns because of my husband, but tattoos can be covered, but I wouldn't want to cover them, they are part of me, a new me."

"A new you?" he quizzed

"New experiences change you. I am who I have met, and I will be who I have yet to meet. My interactions with you will inevitably turn me into a different me,

Master. Are you pleased with them Master?" she questioned him lightly.

"Very pleased, they are impressive."

"I love them all Master."

"Do you slave?"

"I do Master, they and you are now part of me."

"Yes," he said in barely a whisper. "They are, you truly are my property now," his tone held a difference pleasure, almost reverent.

"Yes Master, as stated The Master is: The dawn, The day, The Night."

"I'm your everything slave?" both a statement and a question.

"You really are Master."

"Are you sure?"

"Absolutely Master, you are my universe."

"Am I really?"

"I swore I would never have anyone else's name tattooed on me ever, until you Master."

"And now you have," the pride in his voice clear, taking hold of her wrists he looked intently at one then across at the other, reading the writing. Even though the script was in Latin the meaning was clear. "They look fucking brilliant, but this one I love," bending he kissed it lightly, "you will always belong to me slave no matter what."

"I live to please you, Master. Nothing and nobody else matters."

Spinning her around bending his head once more to capture her lips, he lifted her and placed her in the tub…

"Master," she squealed in delight, "I've still got clothes on," not many she wanted to add.

"It doesn't matter slave they will come off later," he laughed, a deep throaty laugh that sent messages too her brain and her womanhood advising her Master was very pleased with her.

Climbing in after her, Master sat between her legs passing her the soap and cloth, lathering the cloth she placed the soap to one side and proceeded to wrap her arms around him to wash his chest, which was smooth with just a few whisps of hair showing. Bowing her head, she lightly kissed his neck as she cleansed him of the day's dirt, feeling him relax against her she continued to kiss and gently bite down on his neck. It wasn't often she got to brand him but when the chance arose, she took it. The sound of pleasure escaping from his lips was her chance, moving her hand up to the side of his chin she moved his head slightly enabling her to kiss the bottom of his neck, it was his weak point. His Achilles heel if you will. Her kiss becoming more brazen and harsher, his head moving further back, his lips parting to let out a low growl as she bit down to leave her mark on his neck. Her long nails dug into the flesh on his chest bringing blood to the surface.

"Slave," he growled sitting forward and grasping her hands, moving them away from his body, "I know what you have done."

"Master am I not pleasing you?" her voice held feigned innocence.

"I can hear the laughter in your tone Slave," he replied moving her hands aside and standing up.

Steeping out of the tub he admonished her, "Slave you will be punished, now dry me off," he demanded.

Standing she also stepped out of the bathtub, reaching across for the towel that hung on the radiator. Raising it to cover her Master's shoulders she proceeded to towel dry his upper torso, slowly moving down his back planting kisses where the towel had previously been. Master turned and she was faced with his freshly marked chest "shit" she thought to herself Master will not be pleased, she hadn't realised she had dug her nails in so deep.

Looking up his gaze caught hers. "Surveying the damage slave?"

Once more she lowered her head, "Yes Master," she felt she had no recourse to say anything else.

"What have you got to say for yourself slave?"

"I apologise for being out of control Master."

"And?"

"I deserve the just punishment you give for the crime that I have committed."

"Very good slave." He touched the barcode gently running his finger across it. "And what do you think the punishment should be slave?"

"Master," she quietly replied head still reposed, "The punishment is yours to give and mine to take."

"Very well slave," he sighed "I shall be guided by truth, reason, justice and fairness when I give you the suitable punishment to fit this crime."

Lifting her head she gazed into his eyes, once more lost in the cool blueness of them, lost in him. She wanted him to want her as much as she wanted him. It saddened her that she knew no matter what she did or said he never would. He was already in deep with an all-consuming mistress. She may be his slave, but he had a master off his own, a master stronger than him, a master he would never admit to it.

"What's on your mind slave?" he queried

"Just thoughts of how to please you, Master."

He turned and looked at her, "Are you sure?"

"Of course, I'm not sure," was what she wanted to

scream in his face. "Yes Master," was her reply

Just a kiss

The vulnerability clear to see, as you look into my eyes
Your hand on my neck
Your breath close
Trust me your eyes say
I stare in reply, I will, I do
Tighter, tighter, always tighter
Closer, closer, pull me closer
Kiss me softly
Kiss me harshly
Kiss me passionately
Kiss me forever
M/s

He wondered out of the bathroom. "I'll wait for you in the bedroom," he said looking over his shoulder at her, "take off your wet things, bathe and put on dry stockings only."

"Yes Master"

"And slave," he stopped and turned.

"Hair down, make-up heavy."

"Yes Master," she replied to his retreating back

Eyes wide shut

"Open your eyes," her mind was telling her. "No," she replied to herself. Her body felt like it had done ten rounds with Mike Tyson. What the actual fuck? What the actual fucking fuck? Was the final singular thought going through her mind! She wanted to pee, but she was putting it off knowing it would probably hurt, she had read up on urethral sounding but had never experienced it, until last night.

Slowly she opened her eyes, just enough to know that it was still dark out, turning her head she looked at the bedside clock, 4:55am, still early. She closed her eyes once more and turned over willing herself to fall back to sleep, knowing this would be an impossible task, but she would try anyway. Her body clock was still in work mode even though it was her day off. It wouldn't be any good, her mind was awake and active, opening her eyes once more she waited for them to adjust to the darkness, the only light that shone was from the digital clock on the bedside table.

She didn't need the light of day or any other false light to know what the bedroom looked like; it was as devoid of emotion as the rest of her Master's flat. The only bit of human that peaked through were the artwork sketches of him she had created and presented to him. That seemed like an eternity ago now. But that was then, and this was now. She felt a little pride that he had one of her pieces out on display, even it was only for him to see, as there were little or few visitors to his flat, he was a solitary creature at home, work and out. He had a circle of drinking buddies, but she thought to herself were they his friends or merely acquaintances? It was his choice she supposed.

She had always felt that his life has been put on hold the minute his divorce papers were issued, almost like he had placed it in stasis! Waiting.... but waiting for what? Was he waiting for something? Or someone? It would be pointless for her to probe as his answer to such questions would be "I don't know", it always was. She suspected he knew but confrontation wasn't his favourite pastime, not outside of work anyway.

But this was his world, not hers. To her he was her world, not her whole world, that wasn't her personality, but it was his to think he was. She had crossed paths with narcissists before, but none had the strength of personality he had. Was that what she was drawn to? She kept asking herself that question but had yet to find an answer. All she knew was that she had unfinished business with him, and until her mind turned the sign to read closed, she always would. She pondered on what she would be classified as, in his world.

Was she a visitor?

An interloper?

An initiate?

The path was chosen, and she would not stray from it until the journey was completed.

Marked

Owned…what is owned?
Could I ever be truly owned?
Tattoos are seen, a choice, a design of my own making
Independence is within, strong, resolute
Marked is a state of mind
Undaunted by the journey ahead
The path I follow is of my own choosing
Never shall I fear the path less travelled
Only the dark of the wood
Even there the sun shines through at the break of day

©Angie Beastall

She had recently told her lover "Omnes vias iter Fi".

"What does that mean" he had asked perplexed.

"We all have paths to travel Fi, mine has always been the path less travelled, it's how I am. I gather and change along the way."

Gather, she had thought at the time, what did she gather? It was a question she needed to answer before she could move forward from this place that she currently found herself.

"I have no problem with you travelling down any path you desire," he had replied to her. "But I am not your husband…Yet! Don't protect me from the truth. That hurts more than the destinations."

Had she hurt him yet again? The thought ran instantly through her mind! She didn't mean to, but then she never meant to hurt anyone, it just happened.

"I love you, Fi. We are and always will be Fi." Reaching across to touch him. He backed away a little, flinching at her touch, almost like she had burnt him; dropping her arm she continued. "There are things that are dark and deep within me, that I don't talk to anyone about, not even when I'm arguing with myself" she laughed, it wasn't a happy laugh!

"This is a journey I need to face alone," she continued, "it started long ago and even though there are forks in the road, the signposts are clear to read," her voice held the sadness that she felt. "What do you want to know" she had asked "Just ask and I will answer if it's within me"

Looking at him, she waited……

"Do you have a burning question that you would like to ask Fi?" she continued her voice soft, her gaze intense.

He looked straight into her eyes as if trying to reach her soul, she knew she would not lie to him. But is omission a lie? she thought to herself.

"There was a burning question, but I have worked past it."

"Really," she queried, "What was the question and how did you get past it?" she really was interested.

"The question was really for me to ask me and to answer in my head," he shrugged lifting his hands before replacing them at his side.

"Tell me! "Neither a demand, nor a request. Just a statement.

"I told you they were for me, and for me alone to help me get over my paranoia."

"Really," the question intriguing her even more, "So," she continued lightly tapping her index finger against her lips. "You ask the question in your head, give yourself both good and bad answers to enable you to work it through."

"Basically, yes."

"OK," she replied slowly. "So, tell me the question?" this time a request.

"It was a question never intended to be asked," Fi continued to argue.

"Just ask me already," her patience wearing thin.

"OK," he sighed deeply, "but remember this question comes from my paranoia"

"Go on.",

***

She didn't want to think about that conversation any further, she realised as soon as the question was out of his mouth, she would have to dance around the edge of truth. She would never knowingly lie to him, that wasn't who they were. She may omit parts of the answer justifying it to herself with "it would hurt him otherwise" when this was a conversation, she didn't want to have with anybody, not Fi and most definitely not with herself. She would do what she always did play the "I'm so selfish card" and have done with it. Sadness once more enveloped her. Desperation forced her to lift the covers from her naked, marked and weary body. Swinging her legs out the side of the bed, she gingerly stood and started to lightly pad across the bedroom towards the door that led to the bathroom. She really wasn't looking forward to this first pee as she knew it would burn. Sitting down and trying hard to hold it in as much as she could hoping to pee a little at a time, praying that that would solve her problem.

"Slave," her Master's voice suddenly boomed from the bedroom. "What the fuck do you think you are doing?" anger coating his words.

"I needed to pee, Master."

"Come back here this instant slave," he demanded. "You know you and everything to do with you and everything from you belongs to me."

"Yes Master," she replied standing up and returning to the bedroom.

This path was certainly turning into a multitude of new experiences. She knew what the Master wanted she could remember the text conversation like it happened yesterday.

"So," the Master had written, "what's your idea of depraved"

She thought about it long and hard before she replied, what was classed as depraved? She wasn't strait-laced enough for her to call anything depraved if she was truly being honest with herself.

"Golden Showers," was the only thing that popped into her head.

"And how do you feel about them?" he questioned further.

"I have only done them once and wasn't really a fan"

"By you or on you?"

"To me…it's like other body fluids… piss is harsh if you don't drink enough water and semen flavours to your diet."

"Piss really is, what do you mean about semen?" he questioned

"If you eat sweet stuff, it tastes sweet and sour equals bitter."

"Mine should be fine then," he jested as his diet mainly consisted of peanut butter and Nutella

"Do you do golden showers?" she queried.

"I do."

"On you or me?"

"If I'm honest I quite like both."

"OK, add it to the list. My piss tastes fab due to the amount of water I drink."

"Does it really?"

"It does," she texted back, "you can taste it."

"I'd like to."

Master demanded that she returned to the bedroom. Walking gingerly back across the hallway to the bedroom, the cool air bringing goosebumps up on her naked flesh, making her want too pee even more. As she walked through the door, she collided with her Master's bare body. He had gotten out of bed and was stood waiting for her to return. Looking up at his face she knew that he was not happy that she had left the room without first seeking his permission. Raising his arm, he struck her hard across the face knocking her to the floor.

Tears sprang into her eyes as she looked up at him towering over her.

 "Get up," he demanded taking hold of her arm and dragging her to her feet.

Tears streaming down her face, the shock of what had just happened not yet reaching her brain. A sense of déjà vu creeping into her psyche of a time. Of a place from long ago hidden within the depths of her mind. Fighting, clawing its way to the surface, an image bursting into her mind from that time, from that place. Trying hard to suppress it, she squeezed her eyes shut, trying to keep it out but to no avail.

The image of a naked seven-year-old standing in the room of the family home, crying. The tears would not stop, could not stop. She couldn't stop them then as she couldn't stop them now. The brutality too much to bear. Her voice lost to the anguish of the situation. She hadn't wanted to "play" with her stepfather, she never did, but he was the adult and she the child.

The bruises healed. But the scars she would carry forever in her mind. The helplessness she had felt had overwhelmed her. The tears would not stop, she hadn't been able to stop them that day and they hadn't saved her from a savage beating from her stepfather. But they had saved her from being raped once more.

Her stepfather had lost his temper and struck her hard across her face sending her flying. The hatred, and the rage that she felt that day for her stepfather once more bubbled to the surface. She had sworn she would not allow herself to be in that position again. Yet here she was, in that position once again. What had she done? She questioned herself, why had she allowed herself to be subservient to this man, her so called Master? She had become infatuated with him, and somewhere along the path she had lost her direction.

The fire once again building within her. The anger rising to the surface. He would not get away with this. She would make him pay. He was not worthy of her. He never was. Looking down at the tattoo bearing his name, she knew that she had had this one not for him but for her. A self-imposed scar to remind her of why she had chosen this path. The scars we bear make us stronger. He was no longer Master he was just Steven.

"Slave," his voice cutting into her reverie, "lay down on the bed."

Looking at him with her newly unveiled eyes, she saw him for what he really was, for what she had always known him to be, a true narcissist. She had once told him that he was a multi-dimensional person, but his ego outweighed any redeeming features that may be buried deep within.

"Yes Master," she replied as the image of the naked prostrate child was once more tucked away in the far reaches of her mind, but the anger, the anger stayed. It would be her blanket warming her for what lay ahead, not only for her but for him.

The Ego that was the Master would not be pleased.

And as for Steven? Well, he could go fuck himself.

Me, She and I

At the beginning and at the end there is only she

I am who I am meant to be

Me…. always me: Me, she and I

He, him and you a mere illusion

A distraction if you will

She the true Master of deception

He the slave caught in a prison of his own choosing

The walls tarnished; the lustre diminished

The finality to end the words on a page

Me, she and I were the real

Accepting of what is and what was never to be

Realists visiting the realm of narcissism

Freedom comes at the end

To those who are willing

Me, she and I

m/S

©Angie Beastall

Wingerworth Writers' Association Other Works

Short Stories
Man of The House.....................Ashley Lincoln
Homecoming............................Ashley Lincoln

Obsession, Lies and Deviancy Series
The Flame.................................Ashley Lincoln
Hitchhikers...............................Nigel Hare
Cold Meal................................Mia Preso
Foreplay...................................Wingerworth Writers' Association (Members)

Secret Stories Told Series
Just For Her...............................Ashley Lincoln
The Game..................................Mia Presso
Lifting The Curse....Banned....... Ashley Lincoln

Novella
Must Try Harder........................Ashley Lincoln
Me, She and I............................Angela Beastall

Novel
Shouting Down the Darkness....Nigel Hare
All Available on e-book from Amazon

Printed in Great Britain
by Amazon